OPEN YOUR EYES

by Roz Abisch
illustrated by Boche Kaplan

Parents' Magazine Press
A Division of Parents' Magazine Enterprises, Inc.
New York

FOR M.M.K. AND H.R.A.
AND OUR OWN SPECIAL THANKS TO
REMY CHARLIP

One rainy day Tim Small said
To his little brother, Ed,
"We can't go out to play.
Let's play indoors instead."

"What can we play?" Ed asked him.
"Let's play RED," answered Tim.
"What is RED?" asked Ed.

"That's the game! Just what you said.
It's all the things we know are RED.

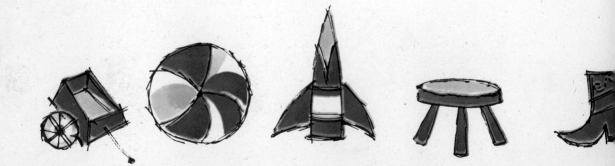

My bed is RED . . .

A is RED, so is a plum,

And the wrapper on my chewing .

An and a 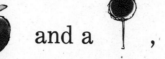 ,

The handle on Mommy's dusting 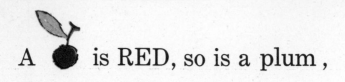 .

My cowboy  ,

My winter ,

The ribbon on our pussy  .

The that's setting in the sky,

My very special dress-up .

The leaves that tumble from the 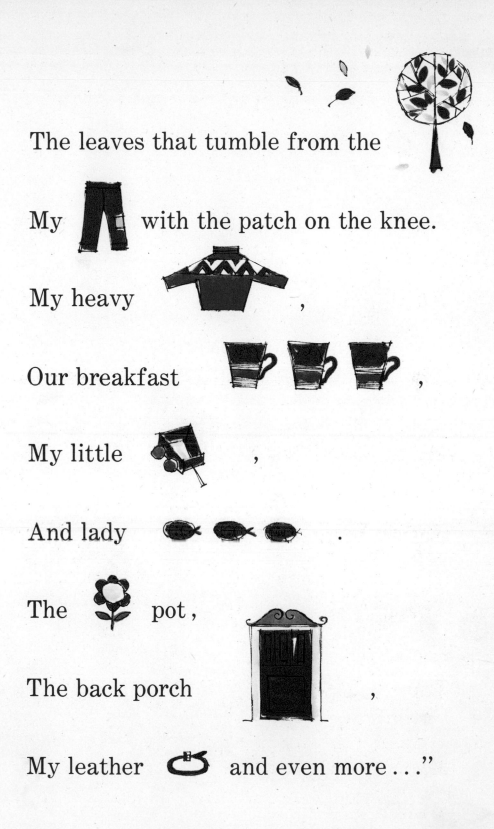,

My 〔image〕 with the patch on the knee.

My heavy 〔image〕,

Our breakfast 〔image〕,

My little 〔image〕,

And lady 〔image〕.

The 〔image〕 pot,

The back porch 〔image〕,

My leather 〔image〕 and even more..."

Then Ed said,
"What else can we do?"
And Tim answered,
"We'll play BLUE."

"All right," said Ed,
"But I'll go first.
I'll tell you what I think is BLUE.

Some fish are BLUE...

Some butterflies, too . . .

And the birds we looked at in the zoo.

Dad's  is BLUE,

So is his ,

And so is Mister Johnson's

My  is BLUE,

My is BLUE,

And so is the   I gave to you.

The  is BLUE.

Or is it green?

I really think it's in between!"

Then Tim said,
"Now it's my turn to play.

I want to play YELLOW.
It's so bright and gay.

My  is YELLOW,

My hoe and my ,

And the candles on my birthday .

A ◆ is YELLOW,

My 🅰🅱 ,

And my 🎺,

And the 🎩

I put on my piece of 🌽.

My  is YELLOW, my

And my ,

And the I wear to bed.

My are YELLOW,

My for the rain,

And my brand new choo-choo

Some fruits are YELLOW . . .

Some flowers in May . . .

Look! The YELLOW sun is shining.
We can go out to play."